GW00726962

• little tales •

Jack
and the
Beanstalk

Retold by Stephanie Laslett
Illustrated by David Anstey

$$p$$

Contents page

* Aladdin & The Magic Lamp
* Alice In Wonderland
* Cinderella
* Goldilocks & The Three Bears
* Hansel & Grettel
* The Little Mermaid
* Puss In Boots
* Sleeping Beauty
* Snow White & the Seven Dwarfs

* The Three Little Pigs
* The Wizard of Oz
* Brer Rabbit & The Riding Horse (and other)
* Peter Pan
* Rumpelstiltskin
* Tom Thumb
* Little Red Riding Hood
* Jack & The Beanstalk
* Wind In The Willows Part I - The River Bank

This is a Parragon Book
This edition published in 2001

Parragon
Queen Street House
4 Queen Street
Bath BA1 1HE, UK

Produced by
The Templar Company plc,
Pippbrook Mill, London Road,
Dorking, Surrey RH4 1JE.

Cover design by Andrea Newton
Printed in Singapore
ISBN 0-75254-942-1

Once upon a time there was a poor widow woman who lived with her only son Jack in a little cottage surrounded by a small overgrown garden.

Sad to say, Jack was a lazy scatter-brained boy but he was very kind and loving to his mother. That winter had been hard and the harsh weather had left the poor woman weak and ill. Lazy Jack did no work upon the land and so they had no food to eat. Soon his mother feared they would starve.

One morning she sat up in bed, pulled the thin blanket around her shivering shoulders and spoke to her son. "Jack, we have no food left in the cupboard and no crops to pick in the field. We have only one thing left of any value. You must take our cow to the market and see if you can sell her."

So the next day Jack set off for market with the cow and he hadn't gone far when he met an old pedlar coming towards him.

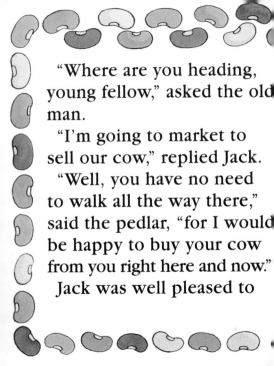

"Where are you heading, young fellow," asked the old man.

"I'm going to market to sell our cow," replied Jack.

"Well, you have no need to walk all the way there," said the pedlar, "for I would be happy to buy your cow from you right here and now."

Jack was well pleased to

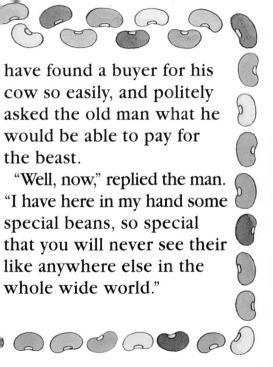

have found a buyer for his cow so easily, and politely asked the old man what he would be able to pay for the beast.

"Well, now," replied the man. "I have here in my hand some special beans, so special that you will never see their like anywhere else in the whole wide world."

Indeed, the beans were very beautiful, all shiny and speckled, and Jack's eyes sparkled at the sight. Thoughtfully he looked at the cow. She was very thin and her bones stuck out most alarmingly. Then he inspected the beans. They were round and glossy and felt very smooth in his hand.

"It's a deal!" he exclaimed and so the old pedlar hobbled off with the cow and Jack ran back home clutching his handful of beans. But when he showed his mother what he had been paid for the cow she was very angry. She boxed his ears and threw the beans right out of the window!

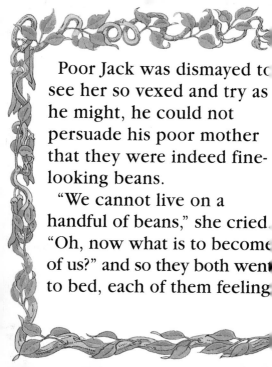

Poor Jack was dismayed to see her so vexed and try as he might, he could not persuade his poor mother that they were indeed fine-looking beans.

"We cannot live on a handful of beans," she cried. "Oh, now what is to become of us?" and so they both went to bed, each of them feeling that all hope had gone.

The next morning Jack awoke to find strange shadows dappling the walls of his room. He ran out into the garden and could hardly believe his eyes. The beans had taken root and grown into a huge plant with thick twisting stalks and quite enormous green leaves.

The beanstalk was so tall that it towered right over the house and, indeed, reached so far into the sky that Jack could not see where the enormous plant ended.

"Come quick, mother!" he called. "Come and see what has grown from our beans!

Together they gazed in silent wonder at the beanstalk

"I wonder where it ends,"
said Jack. "I think I will
climb up and see." But his
mother was afraid of this
strange ladder to the sky
and begged him to stay well
away. Loudly Jack pleaded
until at last she gave in,
then hand over hand, foot
over foot, the curious boy
began to climb the stalk.

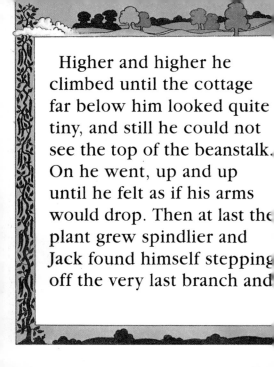

Higher and higher he climbed until the cottage far below him looked quite tiny, and still he could not see the top of the beanstalk. On he went, up and up until he felt as if his arms would drop. Then at last the plant grew spindlier and Jack found himself stepping off the very last branch and onto firm ground. He was in beautiful, lush green countryside and not far away stood a fine castle.

Now Jack's long climb had made him quite hungry, even hungrier than usual, and he would have traded his life for a cool drink of water, so he made up his mind to call on the castle.

He knocked boldly on the great door and soon it swung open to reveal an enormously tall woman. Jack explained that he had travelled a long way and would dearly like a drink and something to eat.

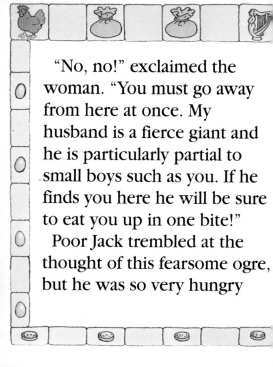

"No, no!" exclaimed the woman. "You must go away from here at once. My husband is a fierce giant and he is particularly partial to small boys such as you. If he finds you here he will be sure to eat you up in one bite!"

Poor Jack trembled at the thought of this fearsome ogre, but he was so very hungry and tired that he begged to be allowed to stay for just two minutes. Then the woman relented, for she had a kind heart, and soon Jack was sitting at a huge kitchen table with a piece of cheese in one hand and a cup of milk in the other.

Just as he was about to take a second bite of cheese, he

felt his chair begin to wobble.
The milk in his cup slopped
over the table top. The
pictures rattled on the
walls and the mugs swung
wildly to and fro on their
hooks. Poor Jack thought a
great earthquake was about
to topple the house when a
loud *thump, thump, thump*
filled his ears.

31

"Quick, quick!" cried the woman, all of a quiver. "The giant is coming and you must hide!"

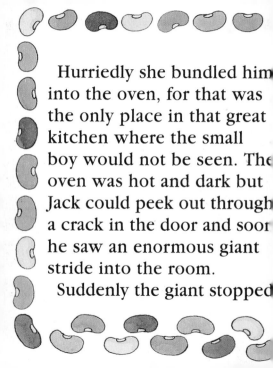

Hurriedly she bundled him into the oven, for that was the only place in that great kitchen where the small boy would not be seen. The oven was hot and dark but Jack could peek out through a crack in the door and soon he saw an enormous giant stride into the room.

Suddenly the giant stopped

and frowned. To Jack's dismay, he raised his head high in the air and sniffed loudly. Then a voice like thunder filled the air.

"Fee, fi, fo, fum,
I smell the blood
of an Englishman.
Be he alive or be he dead,
I'll grind his bones
to make my bread!"

36

"Nonsense!" replied his terrified wife, for she knew she would be in great trouble if Jack was found inside the castle. "You are grown old and stupid. It is a fine fat hog that you smell. There, sit down and eat up your breakfast and let's have no more of your fee-fi-fo-fum." With a suspicious grunt the

giant sat on his huge chair
and began to eat. Greedily
he tucked into twelve
enormous rashers of fine,
fat hog, fifteen fried eggs
and three pounds of grilled
mushrooms, and the meal
so pleased him that he soon
forgot all about the
interesting smell and the
fee-fi-fo-fum.

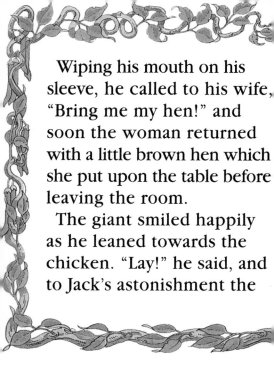

Wiping his mouth on his sleeve, he called to his wife, "Bring me my hen!" and soon the woman returned with a little brown hen which she put upon the table before leaving the room.

The giant smiled happily as he leaned towards the chicken. "Lay!" he said, and to Jack's astonishment the hen instantly laid an egg. But not an ordinary egg. Oh, no, *this* was a golden egg!

"Lay!" said the giant again, and straightaway the hen laid again. Soon a third egg lay on the table. The giant stroked the hen for a while, then yawning loudly and putting his head upon his arms on the table, was soon fast asleep.

Quickly Jack jumped out of the oven and prepared to make his escape — but he was not going to leave that magic hen behind! Carefully he tiptoed across the room and tucked the clucking hen under his arm.

Soon Jack was running from the castle as if his very life depended on it. There was the beanstalk and down he scrambled, all the while holding the hen tightly under his arm.

Soon he was back in his own little garden and his mother wept for joy to see her dear son safely returned. Then Jack put the brown hen down on the ground in front of her and told her of his exciting adventure.

"See, mother," he cried. "This little hen will lay as many golden eggs as we

wish," and with that he said in a loud voice, "Lay!" and straightaway the hen laid a beautiful golden egg. How happy his mother was to see this good fortune after so many years of ill luck.

So they lived for many months and with so many golden eggs to sell, they wanted for nothing.

But after a time Jack grew eager for more adventures and decided he would visit the land at the end of the beanstalk once again. In vain his poor mother pleaded with him to stay and the next day, dressed in a disguise and with his skin stained by onion juice, he set off up the stalk.

Once again he headed
straight for the castle and
as before begged the kindly
woman to let him inside.

The giant's wife was
fooled by Jack's disguise
and did not recognise him
at all. "I dare not let you
in," she replied, "for my
husband is a fierce giant
and would eat you for sure.

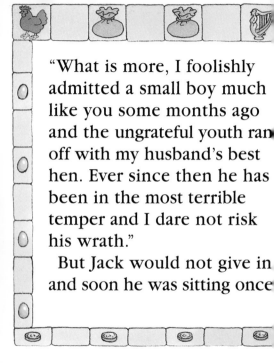

"What is more, I foolishly admitted a small boy much like you some months ago and the ungrateful youth ran off with my husband's best hen. Ever since then he has been in the most terrible temper and I dare not risk his wrath."

But Jack would not give in and soon he was sitting once

more at the giant's table and eating the giant's food. Soon the floor began to tremble and the good woman began to whimper and Jack knew the giant was on his way. Like a flash he hopped off the chair and ran straight to the woodpile in a corner of the room and there he hid safe from view.

With a loud crash the door swung open and there stood the enormous giant with a horrible scowl on his face. Slowly he lifted his nose and sniffed.

"Fee, fi, fo, fum,
I smell the blood
of an Englishman.
Be he alive or be he dead,
I'll grind his bones

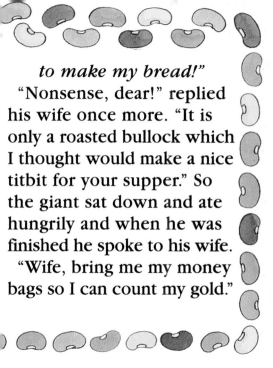

to make my bread!"
"Nonsense, dear!" replied his wife once more. "It is only a roasted bullock which I thought would make a nice titbit for your supper." So the giant sat down and ate hungrily and when he was finished he spoke to his wife.

"Wife, bring me my money bags so I can count my gold."

His wife was soon back with two large bags hanging heavily over her shoulder. With a loud grunt she swung them onto the table top.

"There!" she said. "Now you can count your money in peace for I am going to bed." Then, as the door banged shut behind her, Jack was all alone with the giant.

Jack watched silently as the giant poured a golden stream of coins from each bag and dug his hands in and out of the huge pile for all the world as if he were making bread!

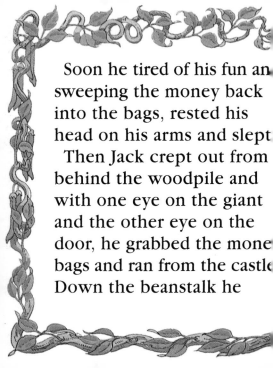

Soon he tired of his fun an
sweeping the money back
into the bags, rested his
head on his arms and slept
   Then Jack crept out from
behind the woodpile and
with one eye on the giant
and the other eye on the
door, he grabbed the mone
bags and ran from the castle
Down the beanstalk he

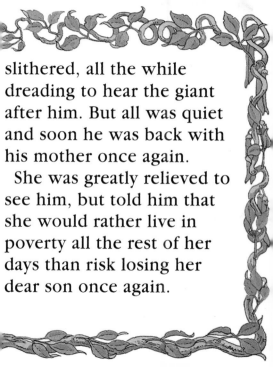

slithered, all the while dreading to hear the giant after him. But all was quiet and soon he was back with his mother once again.

She was greatly relieved to see him, but told him that she would rather live in poverty all the rest of her days than risk losing her dear son once again.

"Fear not, mother," replied
Jack with a merry laugh,
"for see what I have fetched
for you this time." And with
that he upturned the bags
and the golden coins flowed
all over the floor.

And so they lived happily for many more months and not once had to worry about what they might eat the next day. But after a time Jack grew restless and longed for adventure once again. His poor mother's wailing was all in vain and soon Jack was climbing the beanstalk dressed in a fine new disguise.

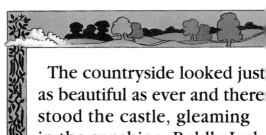

The countryside looked just as beautiful as ever and there stood the castle, gleaming in the sunshine. Boldly Jack knocked at the door and before long it was opened by the kind woman. This time, she was determined to let no visitors inside.

"Some months ago another young fellow tricked me into

letting him stay and as soon as my husband was asleep, he was off with his money bags! My husband never got over it and goes about all day long like a bear with a sore head. You would not wish to meet *him* in a hurry, I can assure you!"

But stubborn Jack would not be dissuaded and his fresh

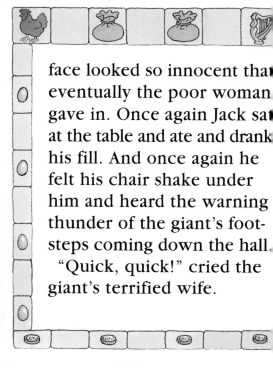

face looked so innocent that
eventually the poor woman
gave in. Once again Jack sat
at the table and ate and drank
his fill. And once again he
felt his chair shake under
him and heard the warning
thunder of the giant's foot-
steps coming down the hall.

"Quick, quick!" cried the
giant's terrified wife.

"Where can I hide you? I shall surely be roasted alive if he should find you here," and she scuttled around the kitchen looking for a hiding place for Jack.

Now it was washday and there by the fire was her large washtub, full of soapy suds and the giant's long woollen socks.

"Jump in here!" cried the woman. "He will surely not think to look in the tub," and so Jack reluctantly hopped into the washtub and laid as low as he could in the soapy water with one of the giant's enormous bedsocks draped over his head to hide him. Then he kept as quiet as a mouse.

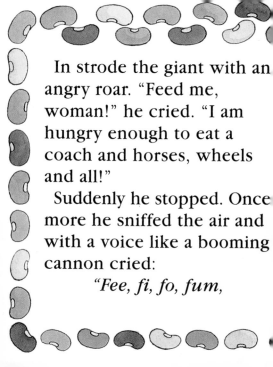

In strode the giant with an angry roar. "Feed me, woman!" he cried. "I am hungry enough to eat a coach and horses, wheels and all!"

Suddenly he stopped. Once more he sniffed the air and with a voice like a booming cannon cried:

"Fee, fi, fo, fum,

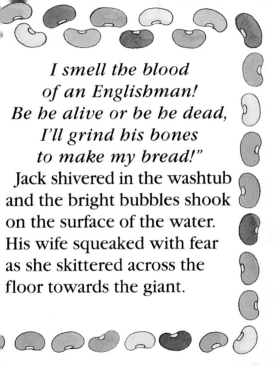

*I smell the blood
of an Englishman!
Be he alive or be he dead,
I'll grind his bones
to make my bread!"*
Jack shivered in the washtub
and the bright bubbles shook
on the surface of the water.
His wife squeaked with fear
as she skittered across the
floor towards the giant.

"D...d...don't be s...s...so s...s... silly, dear!" she stammered. "It is only a tasty sh...sh...sheep I have cooked for your dinner."

Still the giant glowered and snarled. His great head swung from side to side as he hunted for signs of an intruder. Jack froze with terror as the giant slowly crossed the kitchen and opened the door of the oven. Suspiciously he stuck his head inside — and quickly pulled it out again. It was far too hot for anyone to hide in there. One by one, he opened every cupboard in the room and scrabbled in each little corner with his huge hairy hands.

He walked over to the wood-pile and pawed behind the heaped logs. Then he turned and saw the washtub.

"What have we here?" he roared, and the rafters shook.

"Why, dear, it is only washday and I am busy scrubbing your socks," replied his wife, wringing her hands nervously.

The giant's eyes glared as red as coals as he towered over his terrified wife. She pulled her bonnet over her ears and quickly scuttled from the room.

Slowly, very slowly, the great ogre came close to the washtub and Jack squeezed his eyes tight shut. He could feel the

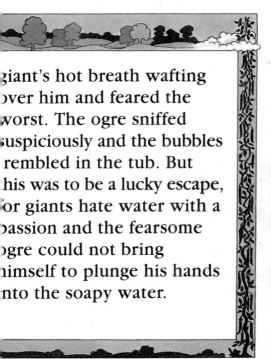

giant's hot breath wafting
over him and feared the
worst. The ogre sniffed
suspiciously and the bubbles
trembled in the tub. But
this was to be a lucky escape,
for giants hate water with a
passion and the fearsome
ogre could not bring
himself to plunge his hands
into the soapy water.

With a disappointed grunt, the giant turned aside and sat down at the table. Jack slowly opened his eyes and breathed a huge sigh of relief to see him tucking into his dinner at the table.

When the giant had finished gnawing the last bone, he pushed the empty dish away and called for his wife.

"Bring me my harp," he bellowed, and soon she arrived carrying a beautiful gold harp, all embedded with diamonds and rubies.

The giant carefully placed it on the table and in a voice that made the rafters tremble he ordered, "Play!" Then to Jack's great astonishment the harp played a very soft,

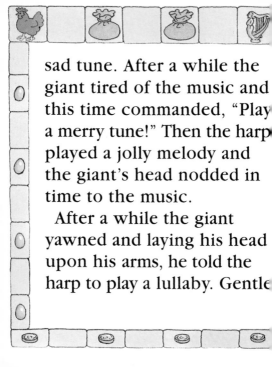

sad tune. After a while the giant tired of the music and this time commanded, "Play a merry tune!" Then the harp played a jolly melody and the giant's head nodded in time to the music.

After a while the giant yawned and laying his head upon his arms, he told the harp to play a lullaby. Gentle

song filled the air and in a
short while the giant was fast
asleep and snoring loudly.

Like lightning, Jack was out
of the tub and across the
room, only stopping to snatch
the harp from the table top.
But what a shock he got
when the harp called out in
a strong, clear voice,
"Master, master!"

With a cry of rage, the giant stumbled to his feet and charged across the room after the fleet-footed Jack. Through the castle Jack raced, out of the door and as fast as his feet could carry him he made for the safety of the beanstalk.

The giant ran after him on his great strong legs, shouting angrily all the while.

87

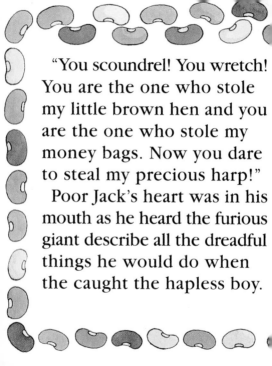

"You scoundrel! You wretch! You are the one who stole my little brown hen and you are the one who stole my money bags. Now you dare to steal my precious harp!"

Poor Jack's heart was in his mouth as he heard the furious giant describe all the dreadful things he would do when the caught the hapless boy.

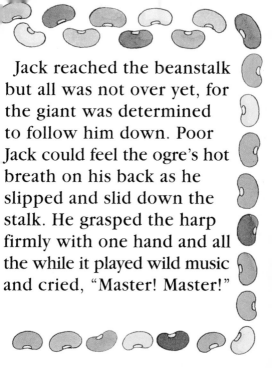

Jack reached the beanstalk but all was not over yet, for the giant was determined to follow him down. Poor Jack could feel the ogre's hot breath on his back as he slipped and slid down the stalk. He grasped the harp firmly with one hand and all the while it played wild music and cried, "Master! Master!"

Behind him the giant crashed and stumbled as he tried to catch the nimble Jack. But the boy was too quick and had soon reached the ground far below.

"Quick, Mother! Fetch the axe!" he cried and his mother came running from the house with the hatchet in her hand. With one mighty blow, Jack swung at the beanstalk and with a great creak and a groan the huge plant began to fall. Then the giant tumbled from its branches.

He landed head first on the ground and was killed on the spot.

All at once the harp played sweet music and Jack held his mother close until she had stopped shaking.

From that time on they enjoyed good luck and great happiness. The hen laid her golden eggs, the harp sang

and Jack, having climbed
the Ladder of Fortune and
discovered that he had
courage and an eager mind,
was idle no more.

JACK AND THE BEANSTALK

The earliest known reference to this old
English folk tale was in 1734 when a satirical
version was published, but the original story
must have been in existence for generations
before this time.

Jack and the Beanstalk became popular
in the early 19th century and had its first
performance as a pantomime in 1819
at Drury Lane, London.